The FLASH
IS CARING

Written By
CHRISTOPHER HARBO

Illustrated by
OTIS FRAMPTON

PICTURE WINDOW BOOKS
a capstone imprint

The Flash is caring. He is kind to others
and concerned for their safety. The people of
Central City can always rely on him for help.

When a storm is brewing, The Flash races to the rescue.

The Flash shows he cares by helping people in need.

When citizens are in danger, The Flash whisks them to safety.

6

The Scarlet Speedster shows he cares by protecting people from harm.

When someone asks a favor, The Flash gives it a whirl.

The Flash shows he cares by doing kind things for others.

When his teammates form a plan, The Flash listens very closely.

The Flash shows he cares by giving others his full attention.

When friends give him a helping hand, The Flash is always grateful.

The Scarlet Speedster shows he cares by saying thank you.

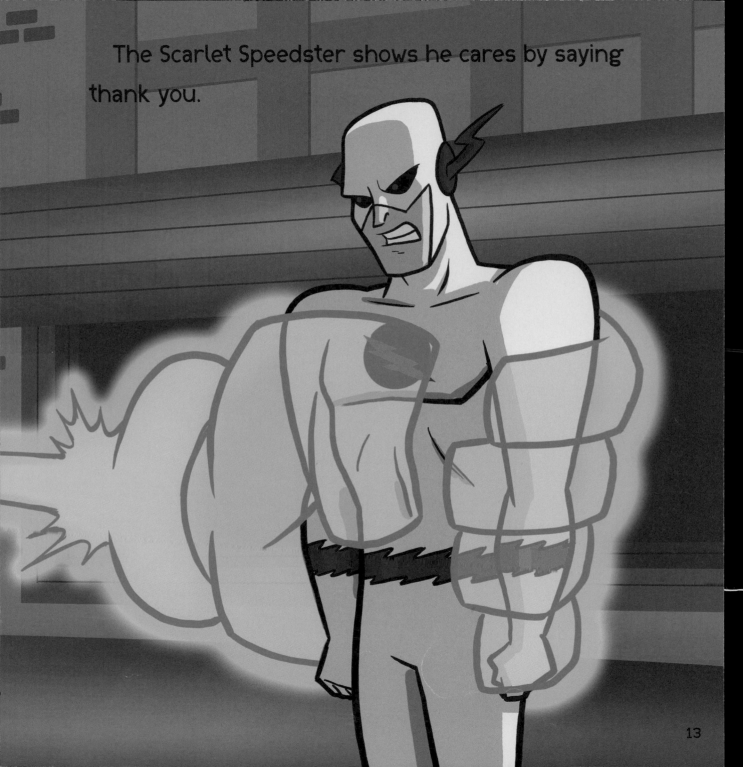

When things don't go as planned, The Flash says he's sorry.

The Flash shows he cares by apologizing for his mistakes.

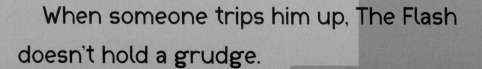

When someone trips him up, The Flash doesn't hold a grudge.

The Scarlet Speedster shows he cares by forgiving others.

When his friends feel down and out, The Flash makes them smile.

The Flash shows he cares by cheering people up.

Whenever super-villains strike, The Flash sprints into action.

And he doesn't care whether they like it or not!

THE FLASH SAYS...

- Caring means helping people in need, like when I give umbrellas to a family during Weather Wizard's attack.

- Caring means doing kind things for others, like when I dry off Supergirl after she saves a puppy from the river.

- Caring means being grateful for help, like when I thank Green Lantern for helping me capture Professor Zoom.

- Caring means apologizing for your mistakes, like when I apologize for messing up a police officer's paperwork.

- Caring means being the best you that you can be!

GLOSSARY

apologizing (uh-POL-uh-jize-ing) — saying that you are sorry about something

citizen (SI-tuh-zuhn) — a member of a country or state who has the right to live there

concern (kuhn-SURN) — to worry

grudge (GRUHJ) — a feeling of resentment toward someone who has wronged you in some way

protect (proh-TEKT) — to guard or keep safe from harm

rescue (RESS-kyoo) — to save someone who is in danger

safety (SAYF-tee) — a condition of being protected from harm or danger

READ MORE

Higgins, Melissa. *I Am Caring.* I Don't Bully. North Mankato, Minn.: Capstone Press, 2014.

Nelson, Robin. *How Can I Help?: A Book about Caring.* Show Your Character. Minneapolis: Lerner Publications Company, 2014.

Raatma, Lucia. *Caring.* Ann Arbor, Mich.: Cherry Lake Publishing, 2014.

INTERNET SITES

FactHound offers a safe, fun way to find Internet sites related to this book. All of the sites on FactHound have been researched by our staff.

Here's all you do:

Visit *www.facthound.com*

Type in this code: 9781515823582

DC Super Heroes Character Education
is published by Picture Window Books
A Capstone Imprint
1710 Roe Crest Drive
North Mankato, Minnesota 56003
www.mycapstone.com

STAR39668

Editor: Julie Gassman
Designer: Hilary Wacholz
Art Director: Bob Lentz

Cataloging-in-Publication Data is available
at the Library of Congress website.

ISBN: 978-1-5158-2358-2 (library binding)
ISBN: 978-1-5158-2364-3 (eBook PDF)

Printed and bound in the USA.
010848S18